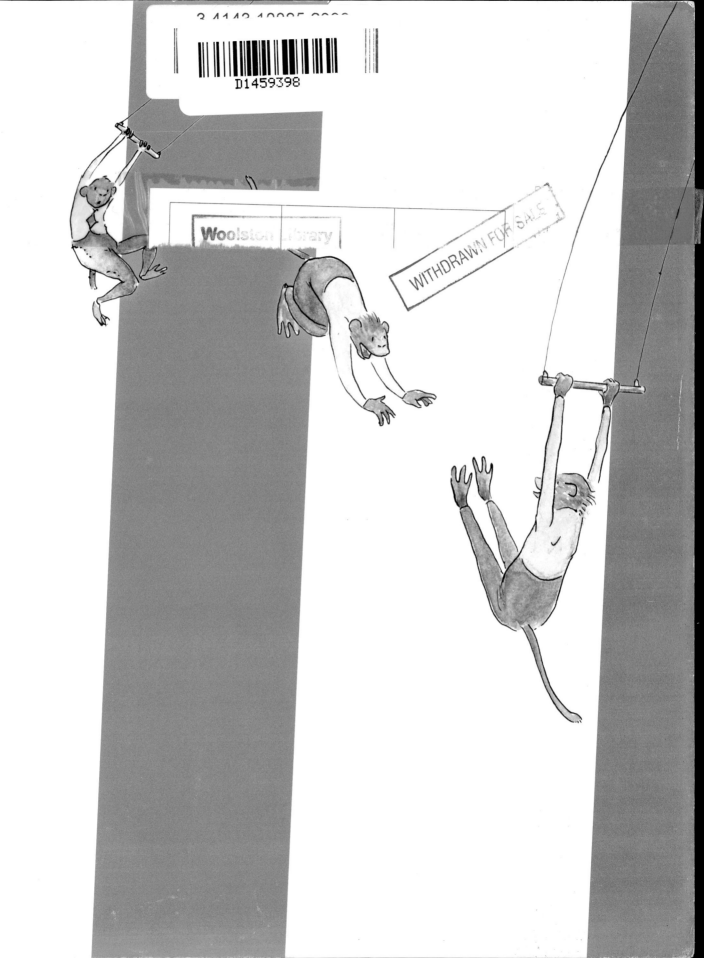

For my sister Christie, with love

Picture Kelpies is an imprint of Floris Books. First published in 2011 by Floris Books. Text © 2011 Lynne Rickards. Illustrations © 2011 Gabby Grant. Lynne Rickards and Gabby Grant assert their right under the Copyright, Designs and Patent Act 1988 to be identified as the Author and Illustrator of this Work.

www.florisbooks.co.uk
15 Harrison Gardens, Edinburgh

The publisher acknowledges
subsidy from Creative Scotland
towards the publication of this volume.
British Library CIP Data available
ISBN 978-086315-843-8
Printed in China

Lewis Clowns Around

Lynne Rickards
and Gabby Grant

Picture Kelpies

There once were two puffins who lived on a rock;
Harris was happy, but Lewis was not.

At dinnertime, Lewis complained with a sigh,
"I hate eating fish, and these cliffs are too high.

The waves make me seasick, the wind makes me spin,
I'm hopeless at flying – I just don't fit in."

As Harris sat thinking his
brother was strange,
Lewis decided he needed
a change.

He thought very hard about
jobs he might do...

A postman?

A teacher?

A guide at the zoo?

Perhaps he could
open a shop and
sell sweets...

Or drive a contraption for sweeping the streets?

Perhaps he'd be happier skating instead,

or painting a picture,

or baking some bread...

"Eureka!" he shouted.
"Hey, Harris, I've got it!
I know what I'll be,
and a puffin is NOT it.

I want to turn cartwheels
and hang upside down.
I'm sure with some practice
I'd make a great clown!"

"You know," replied Harris,
"you might just be right.
You've always been quite
a ridiculous sight.

You trip and you tumble
all over the place,
and everyone laughs at
the sight of your face."

What luck – a big circus had
just come to town!
And Lewis was hoping
they needed a clown.

He flapped very hard
and waved Harris
goodbye.
Although he was
scared, he just
managed to fly.

A brisk wind
was blowing
with worrying force,
but he wouldn't let anything
blow him off course.

Lewis soon spotted
the big stripy tent.
He smoothed down his
feathers and then –
in he went!

"Excuse me," he said to
a monkey in blue,
"I'd like to apply for
a job here with you."

"Go talk to the Ringmaster,
there on that stand.
He's the fox in the hat
with a cane in his hand."

"Hello," said the Ringmaster,
"what have we here?
Speak up, little fellow,
you've nothing to fear."

Lewis jumped up, but before
he could speak,
          he stumbled and bumbled
              and fell on his beak.

"I know if I work hard I'll be a great clown.
Please give me a chance, sir.
I won't let you down!"

The Ringmaster smiled.
"As a matter of fact,
we could use a new clown
in our tumbling act.

Here's Carla Koala.
She's great, I must say,
but we need one more clown – can you start right away?"

Well, Lewis watched Carla hop, tumble and spin,
then jumped to his feet and cried, "Yes! Count me in!"

Next, Lewis met Zorro the Highwire Cat,
the Flying Blue Monkeys, and Daredevil Pat.

The monkeys swung high on their circus trapeze,
which they liked even better than swinging in trees!

KaPOW!

went the canon,
and out poor Pat flew.
The force of the blast
ripped his trousers in two!

Then onto a wire stepped Zorro the Cat,
in his mask and his cape and
his shiny black hat.

The Balancing Pandas showed Lewis a trick –
a pyramid stand that was clever and quick.

They went up in rows
because that's how it's done –
first four, and then three,
and then two,
and then one.

Next one of the pandas jumped up on a ball,
and rolled round the ring with no effort at all.

Another one hopped on a
bike painted blue,
with five other
pandas all
riding it
too!

Well, Lewis was having a fabulous day.
He wanted to start his new job right away!

His new friends all helped him to learn his routine,
and though it was hard, he was terribly keen.

The next day was Lewis's first as a clown,
and he prayed that he wouldn't let everyone down.

He had practised and practised
to get it just right,
and now all that mattered
was opening night...

On with the show – they had no time to lose!
Poor Lewis had stagefright.
Oh, where were his shoes?

He popped on his pompoms
and went through his falls,
while Carla squeezed into her pink overalls.

He pulled on his socks
and his pointy green hat,
and found his big shoes
under Zorro the cat.

"And now," cried the Ringmaster,
"ladies and gents,
I give you the greatest
of circus events!"

When Lewis and Carla hopped into the ring,
the audience roared for their favourite thing...

The clowns had arrived! They both tumbled and spun,
tripped over their shoes and had plenty of fun.

At the end of their act was a special surprise.
Carla stood on a seesaw and covered her eyes.

When Lewis jumped down on the opposite side,
she was going to flip over and whizz down a slide...

But something went wrong,
and she flew much too high!
Up, up, up Carla zoomed –
but koalas can't fly!

The audience gasped.
Was she going to fall?
Poor Carla Koala had
no wings at all!

When her overalls caught on
the monkeys' trapeze,
she dangled there like a
pink sock in the breeze.

"Poor Carla!" thought Lewis.
"Oh, what can we do?"
Then suddenly, though he was
frightened, he knew.

He threw off his shoes and
his pointy green hat,
and was off to the rescue
in three seconds flat!

Lewis fluttered and flapped,
on and on, up he went,
till he got to his friend
at the top of the tent.

He untangled her carefully,
straps in his beak,
trying not to look down –
he felt dizzy and weak.

They floated and fluttered,
a bit like a kite,
with poor Carla dangling
and trembling with fright!

Flying down was a challenge,
but not what he'd feared.
When they both reached the ground
the whole audience cheered!

Then Carla hugged Lewis,
as bears often do,
and Harris came running
to hug Lewis too!

The Flying Blue Monkeys and Zorro and Pat
and the Balancing Pandas all
threw up their hats.

"You're quite a sensation,"
the Ringleader laughed,
but Lewis smiled shyly and said,
"Don't be daft!"

Lewis and Harris flew home to their rock,
and the huge hero's welcome gave Lewis a shock!

He once was a puffin who always fell down,
but now he was famous – a fine circus clown.

His friends crowded round him and lifted him high,
and Harris, his brother, then raised a great cry:

"Hooray for our Lewis,
the bravest of birds!"
And Lewis the puffin
was too proud for words.